HOME FOREVER

ANGIE THOMPSON

Quiet Waters Press

Lynchburg, Virginia

First published in *A Homewood Christmas* October 2022
This publication October 2023

Cover design by Angie Thompson
Photo elements by stokkete, kalozzolak, and korovin, licensed through DepositPhotos
Sheep logo adapted from original at PublicDomainPictures.net

ISBN: 978-1-951001-31-5 (pbk)
ISBN: 978-1-951001-30-8 (ePub)

To Jeremy and Ashleigh, who never let a child feel left out or in the way

Thanks to all the KDWC aunties, who made this project so much fun, and to my awesome cover team as always!

Special thanks to the Studebaker Drivers Club Forum for offering invaluable assistance and direction to this non-car-savvy girl who randomly decided to try to write a competent mechanic!

TABLE OF CONTENTS

ONE

"That bike going to be much longer, Magda?"

The echo of the shop bell followed Mr. Pickett's gravelly voice into the garage, but Magdalen Morris didn't even raise her head from where she sat on a low stool, scrubbing a toothbrush against a grubby bike chain.

"Tell Roger Dykes he'll get it back quicker if he stops letting it lie around in mud puddles." She brushed vigorously at a stubborn clump until it came free, then glanced up, the sparkle of fun in her blue eyes belying her no-nonsense tone. "Better yet, tell him to come in here and see for himself what a little old-fashioned elbow grease will do."

With the sleeves of her navy sweater pushed up above her elbows, a stained towel spread over her plaid jumper, and her short, dark curls tied back in a smart bandana, Magda looked barely older at first glance than she had fourteen years ago, when she first strode into the same room, schoolbooks and lunchbox swinging in one hand, and asked if there wasn't something she could do—just after school and on weekends, "for the war effort, you know, Mr. Pickett," with such a longing look that he hadn't been able to refuse her.

Perhaps that memory was what stirred a grim smile on the grizzled mechanic's face and prompted the quick clearing of his throat as Magda bent over the chain again.

"Wish I could. Save me a heap of work, that's a fact. But it ain't Roger who's waitin' on you, 'less he's split himself into four somehow."

Magda's head snapped up and around to regard the clock on the wall with bewildered astonishment.

"Time already! And I only stopped in for an hour— and Vi's errands only half done!" She shot to her feet, taking time to pat down the half-clean chain and wipe her hands hurriedly on the towel before grabbing up her purse, gloves, and shopping bags from a shelf only half full of spare parts. She flung a distracted goodbye over her shoulder to Mr. Pickett and Clay Warren, who stuck his head out from under the hood of the Quinceys' old Ford to watch her go with a merry grin. Mr. Pickett harrumphed as he picked up the discarded chain, but the corners of his lips twitched again as he sat down on the stool Magda had vacated and took up the brushwork.

Meanwhile, the source of their amusement had stepped out of the cluttered garage and into the equally cluttered front room of the repair shop to be met with excited exclamations from all sides.

"My turn! It's my turn!"

"Oh, Aunt Magda, Andy Burns stole my hair ribbon!"

"I knew we'd find you here!"

"I'm sorry, Aunt Magda; we would have gone straight home, but Dale insisted…"

Magda took it all in with a laugh and a smile, slipping into the worn coat and knitted cap that hung on a peg by the door and leading the procession out of the shop before she bent down to the level of the littlest boy and addressed each in turn as she slowly straightened.

"Of course it's your turn, Dale; I wouldn't forget. Bertie, dear, I'll send an extra cookie in your lunch tomorrow; see if Andy doesn't like that better than hair ribbons. That was clever of you, Ted, to know just where to look! Never mind, Len, darling; I wouldn't miss riding you home for the world. Tell Mother it'll be just a few minutes for Dale and me; I only need to dash into Hanby's to get a few things for supper."

Magda retrieved her bike from the side of the shop and straddled it, holding out her arms to Dale, who was bouncing like a rubber ball in his excitement.

"Up and down, Aunt Magda! Up and down!"

"Oh, Downy, you're getting too big for my arms!" Magda groaned, but she braced her feet and singsonged, "Up hill…and down Dale!" at the same time lifting the five-year-old as high as she could before plunking him down on her handlebars. "Bertie, hand us up that bag, will you?"

3

"I'll take it for you, Aunt Magda. You've already got Dale and the supper things." Ellen held a hand out, and her little sister hesitated between them, but the next second Ted cut in.

"No, I have to take it, don't I, Aunt Magda?"

Magda pursed her lips to hide her smile, and her voice was carefully grave as she answered.

"It's the right thing to ask, Teddy, but a gentleman wouldn't say 'have to.' He should offer willingly or not at all."

"I would very much like to carry the bag, please, Len." Ted turned to his older sister with an air of awkward politeness so comical that his aunt had hard work not to laugh outright, and Len looked utterly lost.

"But Len doesn't have it, Teddy. I do!" Roberta's mystified tone as she stood still clutching the full shopping bag to her chest was the last straw, and a low ripple of laughter finally broke from Magda's throat.

"Give it to Teddy, Bertie, darling—Ted, put your scarf up, dear; it's warmer than this morning, but it's below freezing yet—and run home to Mother, all of you. Or Dale and I might still beat you, even with Hanby's."

"Bet you won't!" Ted yanked at his scarf, snatched up the bag, and shot across the street as fast as his nine-year-old stride could carry him, and Len took Bertie's hand and followed him up as fast as seven-year-old legs and twelve-year-old dignity would allow. Magda watched

4

them for a few steps, then smiled down at the little face turned up to her in anticipation.

"All right, Downy, feet up! Let's ride."

TWO

It was less than a half hour later that Magda's bike found its way off the road and up to a snug Dutch Colonial on the very edge of Homewood. Swinging Dale off the handlebars, she leaned the bike against the porch and scooped the bag of groceries up in one arm, bending down to catch the blur of pigtails and pink denim flying toward her in the other.

"Gracious, Phyl, you'll be on your nose in a minute, racing down the steps like that! It's much too late for cyclone season, you know."

"Dance me, Magga, dance me!" the little girl squealed, joyfully ruffling her aunt's short curls.

Magda dashed to catch the screen door with an elbow as it closed behind Dale, shoved it wide enough to admit both the grocery bag and the three-year-old, and caught it with her foot to keep it from slamming as she set both loads down in the vestibule.

After shrugging out of her coat, rescuing her hat from Phyllis's inquisitive hands, and hanging them both on one of the many hooks along the wall, she snatched up the bag and the little girl again, humming a popular tune as she twirled and two-stepped her way to the kitchen.

"Here, Vi! And I'm sorry—I only meant to stop a minute, but my hands got busy, and…" Magda trailed off with an expressive shrug as she deposited Phyl on a chair and the groceries on the table.

Violet King looked up from the stove with a smile that mingled all the affection of a benevolent sister with the real gratitude of a harried housewife.

"You're a dear, Magda, through and through. I know you'd spend every waking hour at Pickett's if you could, but it's such a relief to know that whatever errand I send you on'll be done when it's needed, for all that."

Magda shook her head with a wry smile as she deposited the change in Violet's little jar and returned to the table to unload her purchases.

"You ought to just be glad that the bus comes in time for making supper. I might never remember to come home otherwise."

Violet chuckled and gathered up a pile of potatoes from the table, pausing at the cutting board when a soft little head butted up against her leg.

"Shall I take the knife or the baby, Vi?" Magda scooped up little Roxanne and held her halfway out, but Violet smiled and waved her away.

"The baby, by all means. She hasn't had nearly enough Magda time today, and I've got supper all planned if I can just have a free moment to carry it out."

"Mother thinks the potatoes will be better without sticky baby fingers." Magda positioned Roxie on her hip and eyed her soberly. "But I think Roxie would have more fun with her birthday blocks anyway, don't you?"

Little Roxie squealed and clapped her hands, and Phyl jumped forward and nearly fell off her chair.

"Me too, Magga?"

"Yes, you too. Ask Dale to bring his Noah's ark down, and we can make a zoo for the animals."

Phyl gave a happy squeal as she hopped from the chair and clattered up the steps, and Violet shot her sister a grateful glance.

"You're a gem, Magda."

"Oh, I'll have as much fun as any of them, and you know it." Magda waved the compliment away as she toted the grinning baby to the living room and brought out the new set of painted blocks, which had only acquired a few faint tooth marks in the weeks since Roxie's birthday.

Phyllis and Dale arrived together a few minutes later with the Noah's ark and set to work sculpting walls and footpaths with the larger set of unpainted blocks that had first been Ted's. Roxie having shown a decided preference for knocking things down instead of building them up, Magda moved her blocks into a corner away from the

9

zoo and patiently built her tower after tower, reveling in the sound of her baby laughter amid the clattering wood.

After a few minutes, Bertie brought in her doll and her reader and curled up on the other side of Magda to practice, and not long after, Ted arrived to take charge of the building project, after dutifully handing over his spelling homework for Magda to check. Len's junior high teachers always kept her busier after school than the younger children, but she finally made an appearance, pausing at the door and eyeing Magda questioningly before her aunt's smile and shake of her head sent the girl on to her mother in the kitchen.

The last block had been carefully positioned, the table set, hands and faces scrubbed, and Violet was casting a worried glance at the clock when a loud rattling in the yard sent the children flocking toward the door. Violet breathed a sigh of relief and hurried from the living room to clear a path for her husband, and Magda followed, utterly unconscious of the thoughtful frown on her face that any of her friends would have known in a moment.

The instant Jim King opened the door, he was beset with eager voices on every side, mostly begging him to come in and look at their creation, but just as he stepped to the door to comply, a devastating crash alerted the whole company that little Roxie had not followed the exodus to the vestibule, choosing instead to take possession of the enticing archway that sat at the very center of the zoo, and leaving fallen walls, broken pavements, and scattered animals in her wake. The howls and tears that followed resisted even the combined ministrations of both Violet and Magda and were finally quieted only by Jim's promise to help rebuild the ruined masterpiece, but not until after he'd had his supper. By then the children's grief had subsided enough to admit the sense of this, and there were no complaints as the family filed into the dining room, although Phyl shot a disapproving glare at Roxie as she was strapped into her highchair.

Magda waited until the last plate was filled before turning to her brother-in-law with the innocent question that had played such a critical role in the late disaster.

"Car giving trouble again, Jim?"

"Afraid so." Jim sighed as he tipped his head back. "It's seemed better all week, but I could barely start it this afternoon, and I all but crawled home for fear it would die completely."

"I'll look at it tonight." Magda nodded as she turned to her plate, and Violet winced.

"In the dark, dear? Can't it wait until morning?"

"It'll be just as dark in the morning, and we need to know what we're up against before we can plan for it. I won't be long, Vi, I promise. The old fussbudget isn't subtle about its troubles; that's one comfort. Use your napkin, Dale; that sleeve's good for another day at least."

Violet sighed and subsided with only the briefest glance of concern toward her husband. But when Magda pulled on her coat after dinner and Jim reached for his own to accompany her, she waved him away with a mischievous smile.

"Oh, no, you're not. You've got a zoo to rebuild. Bertie's night for dishes, isn't it? Then Len, would you come hold the flashlight for me? I won't be long."

A quick look of relief flashed in Jim's eyes, and he allowed Dale and Phyllis to drag him into the living room as Len tugged on her coat and willingly followed her aunt.

THREE

When Magda and Len returned to the house less than half an hour later, the rest of the family circle was gathered in the living room, Jim supervising the construction of a newly expanded zoo from his seat on a chair nearby while Violet kept Roxie's busy little hands out of the way on the couch. Ellen tripped into the room with a lighter step than she'd carried all day, found a seat on the other side of the baby, and held out her hands. Magda entered more slowly, a visible cloud shadowing her usually happy face as she leaned against the wall next to the door. Jim glanced up at her, and a wry smile curved the corner of his mouth.

"That bad, huh?"

"Not as bad as it could be." Magda sighed and slid to the floor, where Phyl immediately crawled into her lap. "But the spark plug wires are completely shot, and there's nothing I can do to fix them. We're going to have to buy, and that's all there is to it."

"Sounds like I'll be taking the bus tomorrow." There was no censure in Jim's tone as he turned back to the children's construction project, but Magda winced.

"I'm sorry I can't have it fixed by then."

"Magda." The little chuckle beneath her brother-in-law's words took some of the sting from the tired slump of his shoulders. "That car's all of fifteen years old, and you've kept it running on determination and spit since Dale was a baby. It's not your fault if a part's so worn through that even you can't patch it anymore."

"Maybe not." Magda shrugged a shoulder, but her tone was unconvinced. "I'm sure Pickett's will have what I need. I'll stop by as soon as he opens. Then I'll bring it in and leave it at Miller's for you."

"And then what? Sit around all day and wait for me or the bus? I can ride it back here as easily as not."

"And miss a perfect excuse to shop in Steadman?" Magda sprang to her feet, giving Phyl a little whirl before setting her down. "That's just like a man. Isn't there anything you want me to pick up for you, Vi?"

"I'll give you a list." There was no mistaking the gratitude in the look Violet sent toward her sister, even as her tone stayed carefully nonchalant. "Christmas is coming, after all."

"Ohh, paper, Aunt Magda! Star paper!" Bertie clapped her hands, and Ted spun around, nearly knocking over the ill-fated wall for a second time.

"And things for cookies! Lots of them!"

14

"We can get all that at Hanby's." Practical Len shook her head at her siblings, then cocked it thoughtfully. "If you're going, Aunt Magda... Will we have another chance before Christmas, do you think?"

"I'm sure we will. Send along anything you need now, but there's still plenty of time to do your own shopping. We should all go up together on a Saturday. Wouldn't that be fun?"

"Magda's idea of fun is most people's idea of a circus." Jim shot a raised eyebrow at his wife, who only smiled as Magda tossed her head.

"And who doesn't think a circus is fun?" She turned to the children, palms up and arms outstretched, and Dale's eyes grew wide.

"Are we going to a circus, Aunt Magda?"

Jim groaned, and Violet shook her head, but Magda only laughed as she settled on the floor next to him.

"No circus, Downy. Don't you think we have all the circus we need right here?"

"Not circus, Magga! Zoo!" Phyl pointed emphatically, and Magda cuddled her close.

"You're right, Phyllie, of course. And a very nice zoo, too. Show me what you and Daddy have done."

The tour of every intricate feature of the zoo had barely concluded when the little guides began to yawn and Violet announced bedtime. The children immediately begged to leave their creation overnight, and when this was quietly but firmly refused, Magda proposed a contest to see if she could corral all of the animals before the combined efforts of the rest could round up the collection of blocks. This done, she took baby Roxie and led the charge up the stairs to supervise the nightly commotion of washing, brushing, and changing into pajamas.

When Violet came to tuck the children in, Magda slipped back to the living room with a stray set of wooden columns rescued from Dale's pockets, and Jim half raised himself from his recumbent position on the couch.

"Don't get up." Magda waved him back, making sure her gaze didn't linger on the heavy artificial leg that now leaned against the wall as she finished returning the blocks to their place. "You've just gotten comfortable, and I'm going back upstairs anyway."

"You know you're always welcome down here, Magda. We're not hiding anything from you, and sleeping upstairs doesn't mean you have to go to bed when the kids do."

"Thanks, Jim. I know." Magda's bright smile showed no trace of the pang in her heart at the tired cast to his face or the thought of the mile walk to the bus stop waiting for him in the morning. "But Roxie never minds my lamp, and it's a perfect time for reading. Unless you'd rather learn about the new Corvette exhaust system than talk with Violet…"

"Oh, get out of here!" Jim swatted the air playfully, the tight line of his mouth relaxing into a grin, and Magda laughed as she ducked back out of the living room, then tossed a kiss to Violet as she passed her on the stairs and made her way quietly to her own room.

FOUR

Humming to little Roxie in the crib that had become nearly a perpetual fixture, Magda quietly made her own preparations for bed and slipped beneath the covers. When the song finished, she waited a few moments for any sound from the baby and, hearing none, turned on her reading lamp. There was something to be said for being the last of six; not much shy of an earthquake would wake Roxie after she had once given way to slumber—a far cry from the way Ted used to stir at the softest footfall.

Magda settled back against her pillows and picked up October's *Car Craft*, one of the few indulgences she allowed herself from what Mr. Pickett sometimes tipped her for helping out at the shop in her free hours, and turned to the article on the Corvette dual exhaust fuel manifold. But she had scarcely made it past the second paragraph when the bottom hinge that she refused to oil gave a little squeak, and Magda looked up to see Bertie's curly head peeking in at the door. She laid down the magazine with a wry little shake of her head, then turned back and patted the bed with a smile, and the little girl scrambled up next to her and cuddled close.

"Can't sleep, Bertie? What's the trouble?"

"Aunt Magda?" Bertie drew a sad little sigh. "Why are boys so mean?"

Understanding softened Magda's blue eyes, and she pulled her niece closer and rested her cheek atop the mound of brown curls.

"You mean the hair ribbon, Bertie-bird? Or are there more boys who've hurt your feelings?"

"No, but Andy used to be nice. He squished a big bug on my desk last week, but when I asked for my ribbon back, he just ran away and laughed at me."

"I wouldn't worry over it too much, darling. Sometimes little boys don't know that little girls don't like to be teased, or to have their hair ribbons stolen. Maybe he's taking it out of his pocket right now and thinking what a nice little girl Bertie King is."

"He wouldn't say that." Bertie shook her head mournfully. "'Cause Miss Holt calls me Roberta."

"Ah. Well, Roberta King, then. Maybe he's thinking how pretty that ribbon looked in your curls today, and wondering if you have another one to wear tomorrow, and thinking how if he tries to pull it again, you'll stick out your lip and scowl at him, and maybe run away, and how you'll be sure to be thinking of him."

"Does he want me to frown at him?" Bertie lifted her head with a puzzled look, and Magda's eyes crinkled at the corners.

"I'm sure he does, dear, because if you're frowning at him, you certainly won't have forgotten him, and that's what little boys care about most."

"Oh." Bertie gave a smaller sigh, then sat back and studied her aunt's face. "Did Daddy ever pull Mother's hair ribbons?"

"I don't remember, Bertie. I was too little when Mother was your age." Magda laughed as she settled down onto her elbow and wrestled a pillow into place beneath it. "You'll have to ask her."

Bertie plopped her head onto the edge of the pillow and turned her round, serious eyes up to face her aunt.

"Did anyone ever pull yours?"

"Of course they did, Bertie-Bobby-bird." Magda swallowed back a sudden lump in her throat and pressed a thumb into the hidden dimple on Bertie's little round cheek, a move always calculated to dent it in earnest. "Why, I lost so many ribbons one month that Grandmother threatened to send me to school with my hair tied in twine if I couldn't keep it in ribbons. Of course, that wasn't all the fault of the boys. My ribbons were forever finding their way into glue-pots or inkwells, or being used to tie something up, but one or two little boys still snatched them sometimes, as I suppose they always will."

"Do they still take them?" Bertie's eyes rounded further, and Magda gave a low chuckle.

"Do I still wear hair ribbons, silly miss?" Magda gently chucked her chin as the little girl shook her head. "I only meant that little boys will keep taking little girls' ribbons until they quit wearing them—and then they'll find some other way to tease. It doesn't mean they don't like you, Bertie. They might even grow to like you very much someday. You'll just have to wait and see."

"Did a boy ever like you very much?" Bertie snuggled her head deeper in the pillow, but Magda suddenly raised herself on her elbow and threw a glance in the direction of the clock.

"So many questions tonight, Bobby-bird! We can't stay up forever talking, you know. You've got school in the morning, and I've got to fix the car for Daddy, so we both need a good sleep. Hurry back to bed, dear, before Len starts to worry or Mother scolds me for keeping you awake. Scoot now!" She dropped a kiss on the round little cheek, and Bertie obediently slid down and hurried back to her sisters.

When she was gone, Magda laid her head down on her arm for a moment before reaching blindly to turn off the lamp, leaving the magazine lying forgotten on the nightstand. No one in the family had ever suspected the sorrow tucked away in a lonely corner of her heart at the memory of one brown-eyed boy who'd had a special affinity for hair ribbons during their days in the little Home-wood school. In fact, she had given little thought to Bobby Thompson once they'd moved to the larger high schools in Steadman, until the winter of her senior year, when he'd approached her at a town social during his one short leave, confessing how lonely he'd been at boot camp and asking if she would write to him after he shipped out. She had agreed—how could she not?—and afterward scarcely a day had gone by that she had not thought of him.

She had quietly posted her first piece of V-mail, truly not meaning to keep it from her sister, but feeling unac-countably shy over the whole idea and finally deciding to wait to tell Violet until she had Bobby's reply in hand. But the reply had never come. In its place had come a dreaded telegram, addressed not to her but to Bobby's parents, informing them that one more precious young life had been cut short amid the horrors of Okinawa. And before Magda had fully absorbed the shock, Violet had received a telegram of her own, announcing Jim's critical injury in Europe, and Magda had thrown herself into the breach, burying her secret grief in a flurry of helpfulness and letting Violet believe the tears in her voice as she sang little Len to sleep were shed for her brother-in-law alone.

Even after the crisis was over, with Jim safely settled at home and her regular part-time work given up for an-other of the returning boys, Magda's sphere of usefulness had hardly seemed to diminish. There was the porch to help convert into a downstairs bedroom, since Jim's new leg was too heavy and awkward to manage the stairs in safety. There were the children—a growing number of them—to pet and look after, especially at nights with their parents out of easy call. There was the car to keep in order, and errands to run, and a hundred more little ways to bring comfort and cheer wherever she turned, and so the years had slipped by, and in the glow of happy busyness, Magda had little time or thought for past sorrows.

But once in a while, the old wound was touched, as it had been tonight by Bertie's innocent questions, and then as now, Magda would bury her head in her pillow, all alone in her room but for the sleeping baby, and let a hot tear or two slip down her cheeks at the memory of a brown-eyed boy and the gnawing ache of what might have been.

FIVE

"You're sure you don't want me to stick around a while, Vi?" Magda gave the hall clock a quick glance as she shrugged back into the coat she'd shed less than half an hour before. "I don't have to go so early, really, so long as I'm there before evening."

"You won't be able to settle until the car's parked at Miller's, and neither will I." Violet's smile mingled love and understanding as she drew Roxie's curious fingers away from the curtain and bounced her gently on her hip. "Besides, I ought to be capable of handling my own house for a day, don't you think?"

"Of course you are, Vi; I didn't mean—" Magda's breath caught, and Violet gave a little groan.

"Darling, of course you didn't mean that. Neither did I. I only meant that there's nothing special I need from you today besides those errands—and fixing the car, of course. You've already done that, so go leave it for Jim and take care of the other, and then take a little time for yourself. I don't know the last time you had a whole day, or anything like it, where someone wasn't pulling or tugging or calling on you for something. Get your hair styled or your nails done or—"

She was cut off by a burst of incredulous laughter from her sister.

"My nails? Truly? I'd break a manicurist's heart, Vi, and you know it." She struck a fashion pose with every finger extended, displaying the short, chipped nails still sporting smudges of grease from her tussle with the car that morning, and Violet shrugged helplessly.

"Fine, then make it a soda or a sundae and a stroll along a new car lot. But take the day and enjoy yourself. I don't want to see you home before Jim is, no matter what."

"Which only really means that I'm not allowed to stow away under the school bus." Mischief danced in Magda's eyes as she tucked in the ends of her scarf, addressing herself to Phyl, who was busily examining her low-heeled pumps. "I know better than to try to walk the distance in these, don't you?"

"Pwetty, Magga!" Phyl stuck her own little feet into the shoes and took a few shuffling steps, and Magda shook her head.

"Exactly that, Phyllie, and not much good for anything else. But since Mother won't let me wear loafers to Steadman, I suppose I'm stuck with them."

"You poor thing." Violet's tone held not a drop of pity. "What would you do with a pair of real heels, I wonder?"

26

"Fall on my nose, most likely." Magda reached out a hand to steady Phyl as she threatened to do just that. "You wouldn't be that heartless, would you, Vi? I won't complain about the pumps again. I promise."

"Better not." Violet raised a brow in warning, but her eyes twinkled, and Magda grinned as she swung Phyl out of her shoes and slipped her own feet into them. Violet scooped Phyl onto her other hip and nodded toward the door, holding both little girls up to the window, where they immediately pressed their faces against the glass. "I'll see you tonight. And your stockings had better be intact."

Magda offered a laughing salute, then hurried out to the car, waving to the three in the window as they disappeared from view, then to Esther Middleton and Peggy Johnson as she passed them on the street, and finally increasing her speed when she reached the main road that connected Homewood to Steadman. Violet was right about one thing; she wouldn't have been able to rest until she'd returned the car to Jim, even if it meant sitting alone in the parking lot until Miller's Furniture closed.

Not that she was in any real danger of having to wait in the parking lot. There were Violet's errands to be done, for one thing, and a few small surprises she wanted for Christmas, and there was bound to be something she'd enjoy doing in Steadman, even if beauty salons formed no part of it. Though if she hadn't been bound by a direct command from Violet and had seen some way to return

27

home before the school bus, she would have been sorely tempted to take it.

But even as the thought crossed her mind, Violet's quiet words rose up to shame her. It was so easy to feel needed in her sister's home—had been since Jim shipped out just after their wedding, when Magda was still in high school. She had tried so hard to be careful—to support and not usurp Violet's role, to bolster and not undermine Jim's self respect, to defer to their authority always, especially when it came to the children. But perhaps she had taken on too much, if Violet felt the slightest need to assert her independence, or perhaps Magda had begun to feel herself a little too necessary, if she couldn't take a day away without worry.

Drawing a deep breath, Magda let her shoulders relax and reached for the radio knob before remembering that it had finally given up the ghost two months ago, or at least passed beyond the limits of what she could repair with used parts Mr. Pickett could sell her at a bargain. She should check while she was in town; the parts to repair the radio weren't the kind of necessary expense that would justify a dent in the family budget, but they would make a wonderful Christmas gift if she could manage it.

She was in the middle of trying to calculate prices and decide what she could give Jim instead, if her limited funds wouldn't hold out for the radio, when her attention was caught by a car stopped on the other side of the road. The bright red color was the first thing to draw her notice, followed quickly by the unique features of the build—a Studebaker from the body shape, but one of the newer models: the kind she had read about but never actually seen in person. But although the car would have attracted her at any time, it was the woman waving frantically from beside it that made her search for a wide spot in the road and turn back in the direction of Homewood, or whichever larger town beyond it the stylish coupe was headed for.

SIX

The woman was at her door before Jim's old De Soto had come to a complete stop, and only after Magda had opened it a crack did she back up far enough to let her slide out. A keen observer would have put the well-dressed, auburn-haired woman at close to a decade older than Magda, though style and makeup had been cleverly employed to mask the fact.

"What's the trouble?" Magda shot a quick look at the stranger before taking a few steps forward and sending an appraising glance over the shining red coupe.

"I only wish I knew!" The woman threw up her hands in dismay, and Magda noted an accent to her words that might possibly have been eastern but certainly was not local to this part of Minnesota. "Is there anyone on this pitiful excuse for a highway who can tell one end of a car from the other? Or could you drop me where I could telephone someone who can?"

"Were you driving when it died?" Magda slipped off her gloves to lay a hand on the hood, and the other woman quickly moved to flick it away. Magda crossed her arms, but the corners of her lips twitched up. "I happen to know a hood from a trunk, ma'am. And a fuel pump from a spark plug from a radiator hose, come to think of it. Would you like my help, or shall I drive you into town so you can wait until the mechanic has time to tow it for you, after he asks why on earth I didn't at least find out what the problem was while I was here?"

"You're...a mechanic?" The stranded driver blinked rapidly, and Magda shook her head as she let her grin blossom.

"I don't work for the shop anymore—not officially. Only because there are men with babies to feed who need the job more than I do. But I've had my hands on nearly every car in town at some point, and if I can't find what's wrong, I can at least save you a little time by telling them what isn't."

"Go ahead, then." The woman's expression hovered somewhere between amused and skeptical as she took a step back and let Magda lift the hood.

After a few probing questions, Magda returned to Jim's car for the toolbox and a blanket, which she spread over the fender before reaching in to remove the distributor cap.

"You don't *look* much like a mechanic, I must say," the older woman commented, and Magda briefly considered rolling her eyes.

"I wasn't exactly expecting you, ma'am. And my sister would die of mortification if I went to town in coveralls, no matter how many stranded motorists I might meet on the way. I'd also rather not test her patience with runs in my stockings or oil stains on my good coat, so you'll have to put up with the pumps and blanket, I'm afraid. When was the last time you had your points set?"

"My what?" Her tone sounded almost offended, and Magda straightened as she turned to face her, barely catching herself before sticking her hands on her hips.

"I'm talking about this beautiful car. Starliner, isn't it? '53? When did you buy it? New, or recently?"

"New, of course. As soon as it was offered. The European look is simply to die for."

"And what kind of care have you taken of it? Not the outside—I can tell you keep it washed and waxed to a shine. But how many times has anyone even lifted this hood in three years? Let alone a qualified mechanic?"

"It hasn't needed it."

"Hasn't it?" Magda sighed as she bent back over the engine. "We'll see if you believe that when I get it running *properly* again. Do you have a matchbook?"

The woman produced one, and Magda tinkered for a moment more before gathering up the toolbox and blanket and then closing the hood with an affectionate little pat.

"All right. Try it now. If we were at the shop, I'd want to set them more carefully, and check the timing too, but

I don't have the tools for that here. Just please, let a mechanic look at it sometime soon. You'll get so much better use out of it if you don't ignore the parts you can't see."

The older woman slid into the driver's seat, and the coupe sprang to life with a roar, but as Magda turned back to Jim's sedan, the other driver sprang out again, faster than Magda would have thought possible in her tight pencil skirt, and clasped her arms.

"You genius! That's the fastest I've gotten it to start in months! I thought it was just getting old and I'd need to replace it before long, but if five minutes' fiddling accomplished that—"

Magda huffed, as much at the thought of Jim's '40 De Soto as the idea of abandoning the beautiful Studebaker for such an easily repaired part.

"Your car's got *plenty* of life left in it, ma'am, and you'd be amazed at what a regular tune-up can do to keep it that way. If nothing else, you'll get much more value out of it when you go to sell if you keep it in good repair."

"And you could do all that?"

"In a garage, yes. I don't have nearly the right kinds of tools here."

"Well, I fear I've been extremely rude." The woman's smile flashed suddenly, and she offered a hand. Magda held up her grease-spotted one with a little grimace, but the woman only laughed and shook it anyway, seeming to give no thought to her expensive gloves. "I'm Ilene

Carmady. Of New York. Touring the country for change and inspiration, and I thought I'd taken a wrong turn out of Minneapolis, but perhaps it's ended up being the right one after all."

SEVEN

"I'm Magdalen Morris." Magda stepped to the back of Jim's car to replace the toolbox and blanket, and the other woman followed her. "I've lived in Homewood my whole life and never been farther than Minneapolis, but I do love cars, and yours is a beauty."

"Is Homewood the little town I just passed through?" Ilene looked back in the direction of Steadman, and Magda chuckled.

"No, ma'am; not if you came from that way. Homewood's ahead of you. Steadman's the city to us, and I'd probably never have gone past it if Jim—that's my sister's husband—hadn't lost a leg in the war and been shipped to Minneapolis. Vi couldn't leave the baby, of course, and she couldn't well look after both of them without help, so there I was."

"And so Minneapolis is the outer limit of your ambition, is it?" Ilene's eyes twinkled with amusement. "What did you think of it?"

"I'd never seen so many people in one place in my life. Or such tall buildings." Magda shook her head. "But I didn't pay that much attention. I was too busy thinking of Len—and Vi—and Jim…" Her voice trailed off, and she swallowed a lump in her throat. "Well, if I ever go back someday, maybe I'll have more time for sightseeing."

"Wouldn't I just love to see your eyes pop at the sight of New York!" Ilene laughed a little harder than Magda thought necessary. "And what did you do after the war, then, when the boys came back to take all the jobs? Marry and settle down with a family?"

Magda looked away, unwilling to show this stranger the deepest secret of her heart, but between her talk with Bertie the night before and the memory of the long days spent in Minneapolis, the thought of Bobby was too close, and her eyes filled with tears. The older woman sighed and put an arm around her shoulders.

"I've done it again, haven't I? Pried too deeply into what's none of my business. Rest assured, Magdalen, I'm the last one to lecture you about *needing* a man. I've done perfectly well on my own for more years than I'll admit to the world." One side of her mouth quirked up, and she stepped back with a last little pat. "But I like you, Magdalen Morris. And since I'm looking for change and inspiration, I'm curious to know what a girl of your talents finds to do in a little town like the one I haven't even seen yet."

The humor in her tone was infectious, and Magda smiled as she looked up again.

"Oh, I keep busy enough. The repair shop has more work than they can handle, and I can always make myself useful there for an hour or two. And one of the family—Vi and Jim's, I mean—is always needing a playmate, or an errand run, or an extra set of hands, or petting or scolding, or an aunt generally, you know."

"And which were you on your way to when I so thoughtlessly flagged you down?" Ilene's tone stayed light, but her nose wrinkled a bit, although she refrained from curling her lip. Magda shook her head with a sigh.

"Just a few easy errands, and then Vi's forcing me to take the day for myself in Steadman after I drop the car off for Jim. He would've taken it this morning except that the spark plug wires gave up the ghost last night, and I couldn't get them replaced before Pickett's opened."

"Well, I'm rather glad of it for my own sake, if not for his." Ilene shot her a wink before raising a perfectly shaped eyebrow. "And you have to be forced to take a day for yourself in the 'city'? What would you rather do?"

Magda shrugged and gave a little wry smile.

"I probably need it if I don't want to take it, don't I? I'd rather be doing something useful, that's all—anything, for anyone, really. Maybe it's selfish, but—I do like to be needed."

"Do you?" Ilene tapped a finger to her lips, and her eyes began to dance. "What time does your Jim need the car then? By noon?"

"Oh, no. He takes his lunch. Just by evening. It's such a long walk from the bus stop, and with his leg…" Magda trailed off, but Ilene hardly seemed to notice.

"Then how would you like to give my car that tune-up you recommended? At the garage, as you said, and of course I'd pay you. Then I'd like to treat you to lunch somewhere—just as a thanks for stopping to help a stranger—and I could follow you into Steadman and bring you back anytime you say. Wouldn't you like a ride in the beautiful car you just saved from an awful death on the scrap heap?" She ended with a laugh and a friendly squeeze of Magda's arm, and Magda's eyes grew wide as she tried to process the breathtaking offer.

"Oh, I couldn't! It's too much. I mean—not that I wouldn't love an hour under that hood, but—"

"But what? Your sister wouldn't approve? You're a grown woman, Magdalen, and she did tell you to enjoy yourself today, didn't she? Not that you'd ever catch me poking around a grimy engine, but if it's what you really want to do…"

"With a little more money, I'd be almost sure of the radio…" Magda's thoughts flew in disconnected snatches, unconsciously muttered just under her breath. "And I could get a hat to match the dress for Bertie's doll…maybe even help with the children's bracelet for

40

Vi…save Jim the extra…and wouldn't I just love to pamper that beauty! But it might not be quite fair to Mr. Pickett…"

"If that's what's bothering you, I'll pay extra for the use of his garage." Ilene lifted her head with a triumphant smile. "But I'm not letting anyone poke around under the hood except you."

A look of almost motherly tenderness crossed Magda's face as she glanced toward the shining coupe, then a smile touched her lips and she nodded.

"In that case, you're right. Vi did tell me to find something I'd enjoy. I'll show you the way."

EIGHT

It was close to noon when Magda once again piloted the De Soto out of Homewood and toward Steadman, after changing out of her borrowed coveralls, restoring her hair to a state that Violet would have called good enough for town, and scrubbing her hands until they were pink in an effort to remove the tiniest traces of oil and grease. Perhaps her morning hadn't been quite the change from normalcy Violet had anticipated, but it had certainly been eventful, and with the generous tip in her purse and the gleaming Starliner purring contentedly on the road behind her, Magda couldn't begin to claim that it hadn't been worth it.

Ilene Carmady had improved her time in Homewood as well, and Magda had overheard enough snatches of her conversation with Mr. Pickett and Clay when she returned from the cafe to know that the visitor had gathered quite a stock of information on the town and its residents in general—and possibly on the King family in particular. But gruff old Mr. Pickett hadn't offered any arguments, even under his breath, when Magda had begged the use of his tools for her project, and he had given them one of his rare smiles when they left. All in all, the small town had extended its plain, hearty best to their unexpected visitor, though just how much of it was for Magda's sake neither woman would have been likely to guess.

It was barely past noon when the two cars pulled into the parking lot of Miller's Furniture, just off the main street in Steadman. Magda had expected Ilene to wait for her outside, but instead the older woman entered the store and followed her back to the little coatroom where Jim generally took his lunch. Jim glanced up when they entered and quickly pushed to his feet, and Magda tried hard not to wince. Ordinarily, she would have taken a seat before he had time to stand, but with a stranger in the mix, the maneuver would have been awkward at best and outright insulting at worst. Instead, she held out the keys, silently resolving to keep their visit as brief as possible.

"Done and waiting—and maybe it'll give us another month or two before something else goes wrong."

"Maybe in another month or two someone'll have a used one for sale at a price we can almost afford." Jim's words were more jesting than hopeful, and Magda grinned as she dropped the keys into his hand.

"And in a size that mostly fits the family, and with parts that don't need much overhauling?" She took a half step away, then paused. "Oh, and don't wait for me tonight. Ugh, my manners! This is Ilene Carmady, and

44

she's insisted on driving me around the city and then taking me home. Ilene, my brother, Jim King."

Ilene shook the offered hand with unexpected firmness, and Jim's eyes widened a little, but he gave her a polite smile.

"That's kind of you, Miss Carmady. Are you staying in Homewood?"

"Not for long." Ilene gave a laugh that might have been pleasant or not depending on the mood of her listener. "But Miss Magdalen did me a good turn this morning, so I'm honor-bound to repay it if I can."

Jim shot a closer glance at Magda, and his grin lit his eyes again.

"Another breakdown on the road? And I'm guessing you washed up before you fixed your hair?"

"Oh, no—where?" Magda's hands flew to her face, and Jim held out his handkerchief.

"Forehead. Right where you swipe your bangs back. Doesn't show if they fall just right, but..." He let his words trail off with a chuckle as Magda scrubbed vigorously at her forehead, then pushed her bangs up for inspection. "You got it. Save you one lecture from Vi, at least. I won't ask about the state of your dress." He winked, and Magda wrinkled her nose but resisted the urge to stick out her tongue as she returned the handkerchief.

"My dress is perfectly fine. I think. We should go, though; I'm ravenously hungry, and you haven't finished your lunch either. I'll see you tonight. Don't work too hard!"

"I'll tell Mr. Miller it's your fault if I don't!" Jim's laughing reply followed them out of the little coatroom, and the echo of it kept the smile on Magda's lips until the door of the shop closed behind her, when she let her shoulders droop with a little sigh.

"Now what's that for?" Ilene swatted at her playfully and motioned to her own car, and Magda bit her lip as she slid into the coupe and ran a finger absently over the shining trim.

"I only wish there was a job that didn't keep him on his feet all day. His leg still hurts him so much at times, and the new one's so heavy and awkward. He's worn out by the time he comes home, but he tries so hard, for the children."

"That's ridiculous." Ilene shook her head as though to scatter the entire notion. "They've made enormous strides in artificial limbs in the last decade or so. Why, I've read of people in much more arduous professions— mail carriers and such—who use them as easily as anything. They're nothing like those awful wooden pegs of the past."

"Wouldn't I love to find a way to get Jim that kind?" Magda's tone held a wistful note as she let her eyes drift out the window. "Or even just a new car that would take one constant worry off his mind. With six children plus

Vi and me, it takes so much just to put food in our mouths. I wish there was more I could do to help."

Ilene opened her mouth and half turned toward Magda, then closed it again, and her brow furrowed as she watched the younger woman. However, their arrival at Steadman's best restaurant brought her out of her curious silence, and she filled the lunch hour with sparkling descriptions of the most spectacular places she'd traveled, which Magda listened to with evident interest. But if Ilene had harbored any thought of arousing jealousy or discontent in her new acquaintance's heart, she must have been disappointed, as by the time the meal was over, Magda remained, by all appearances, as perfectly content with her small-town lot as if a broader horizon had never been opened before her.

NINE

After lunch came shopping, and when Violet's few
cursory purchases were made, Magda set forth on her
own errands with an enthusiasm that might have de-
voured her unaccustomed wealth within moments if not
for the years' worth of frugal habits that now stood her in
good stead. The necessary parts for fixing the radio were
hunted up, a stylish hat and matching coat purchased for
Bertie's doll, and not an insubstantial bit added to the account for Violet's bracelet. The small assortment of nuts,
candies, and colored sugars she'd already planned to
coax from her meager savings received a slight increase,
as did the little pile of decorative paper, and when Magda
finally sank down on a bench with even more of a sparkle
in her eyes than they'd held before, Ilene turned on her
with mock sternness, demanding to know what it all
meant anyway, and why on earth she hadn't bought a single thing for herself.

"Oh, I have!" Magda gave the shopping bag next to
her a little pat as she smiled down at it. "I'll help with the

baking, of course, as much as the children will, and with making stars for the tree—Moravian stars are a Homewood tradition, you know, and we always have them on our tree, as many as we can make. And I'd been worried over Jim's present, but fixing the radio will be perfect. I've already bought for the rest, but Bertie's has been worrying me a bit—one little doll dress didn't seem like much, even if it was especially pretty, but now it's all right. And as for the children's present for Vi, they never could have bought it on their own, the dears, but Jim can always find something to do with the little I've saved him, if he doesn't need it for the matching necklace or brooch I'm sure he's already picked out."

"I don't see how he can justify buying jewelry when you're slaving over his car and his children." Ilene's lips pulled into a tight line, and Magda glanced up, startled.

"Why, it's Christmas, you know. Of course we're saving for another car—have been for years. It's just that some new expense always seems to pop up just when we're making real progress. But putting a few extra dollars aside for something we couldn't see or touch—that's not any kind of present, really. I'd rather have Christmas—but I'd much rather give it."

"I do believe you'd much rather give anything to anyone than take something for yourself, Magdalen Morris!" Ilene sat back and studied her as if she were some new specimen of landscape. "Come now, confess! If you hadn't had the car to return today, what would you have been doing?"

"Watching the little ones while Vi did housework, most likely." Magda tried to answer easily, but a blush crept into her cheeks. "Then in not too long, I'd meet the school bus and help with supper or homework until Jim came in. Oh, but we'd have to stop at the Johnsons' first—since it's a Friday and December now, there are sure to be cookies, and Bertie certainly wouldn't let me forget. That's the best part of the day, really—riding one of them home on my bike and having time to talk—really talk—about their day or their week. Even Len still loves it, although I sometimes walk the bike with her now. And it's something Vi likely couldn't do, if I didn't, so I never have to worry about overstepping."

"Overstepping?" An unpleasant note had crept into Ilene's voice, and Magda bit her lip.

"Taking Vi or Jim's place, you know. Not that they've ever said so, but—I'm not really sure they would if they felt it. They've always made me part of everything, and it's just so natural for the children to turn to me some-times—or for me to start planning for everyone. Of course I love it, but I never want to take what's theirs by right."

The older woman pursed her lips and seemed to swal-low back the words on her tongue, but a moment later, her mouth curved in a slow smile.

51

"I believe I'm starting to see what you mean. You've lived with them for a long while, haven't you? The woman at the cafe seemed to think so."

"Oh, yes." Magda's laugh was a little absent, as though her mind had wandered far away. "Vi and I grew up in that house. Mother died when I was fourteen, and Vi married Jim the same year—just after Pearl Harbor, you know—so of course they kept me then. And there really wasn't anywhere else to go—and they always said they were glad to have me."

"Shocked, I'm sure," Ilene muttered under her breath, but she smoothed her face into a smile again when Magda turned to her inquisitively. "Of course they did. What sister wouldn't? But it must have been rather hard on them—after the war, of course—a young family just starting out, with an extra mouth to feed."

"I know it." Magda dropped her eyes, and her voice fell to a murmur. "I can only hope what little help I can give is worth the expense."

"Oh, I'm sure they would say it was." Ilene lifted her gaze to the ceiling for a moment, as though considering, before bringing it slowly back to Magda. "They know how much you want to feel needed, after all. And it would be rather hard for them to turn you out, with no prospect of a job or…other opportunity…in your future."

Magda swallowed hard and bit her lips together as the thrust hit home, but before she could form a reply, Ilene suddenly jumped to her feet.

"I have a wonderful idea, Magdalen! Come with me. We're going window shopping."

TEN

The window shopping that Ilene had in mind was un-like anything Magda had imagined. It consisted of a stroll along Steadman's new car lots, inspecting not the stylish coupes and convertibles but the rows of large sedans and station wagons, and talking over the features most neces-sary in a family car in general and a car for the King fam-ily in particular.

It was a bit of a dangerous game, one she would never have started with the children for fear of breeding discon-tent, but under Ilene's persistent prodding, Magda al-lowed her mind to turn from the adequate to the ideal and finally permitted herself to pick out the best of the offer-ings—the one she would choose if money were no object or, according to Ilene, "if a rich aunt left you a windfall."

"There, I knew you could do it!" The older woman's eyes sparkled as she leaned back against the car, cutting a rather odd figure with her stylish clothing and carefree attitude next to the sturdy, practical wagon. "Now, I have a proposition for you. How would you like to give this car to your family for Christmas next year?"

"Oh, wouldn't I?" Magda gave a little laughing sigh as she ran a finger along the trim. "But of course I can't, so what's the use of pretending?"

"There's no pretending involved. I'm deadly serious. You could earn this car by next year, and I'll tell you how."

Magda gave her a half curious and wholly disbelieving look, and Ilene raised her perfectly arched eyebrows, but a smile touched the corners of her lips.

"Don't believe me? Here it is, then. I'd intended to complete this tour of the country on my own, but I like you, Magdalen Morris. I'm finding it's rather difficult to converse with a radio, for one thing, and who knows what kind of freak my car might take into its head next—or how some unscrupulous mechanic might try to rob me? Besides that, I want to see your eyes pop at the sight of the Rockies, and the Everglades, and the New York skyline. There's so much more to the world than this one little corner—so many opportunities for a girl with your ability, and I want you to feel that."

"What…what are you saying?" Magda's voice was a little faint, and she took a half step backward as if to brace herself.

"I'm saying that I want you to come with me, Magdalen. Call yourself my personal mechanic, traveling companion, whatever you like. Come with me for a year, and when that's over, I'll bring you right back here and buy you any car you choose, no questions asked. Then of course, if you'd like to give it to the family…"

"Ohhh." Magda let out a quivering sigh, but her head began to shake. "Oh, I couldn't."

"And why not? You're a grown woman, not a child any longer. There's nothing to stop you from doing exactly what you want. And I thought the car was your dream, but of course if you'd prefer something else—"

"Oh, no! The car's beautiful. It's exactly what I'd choose to give them if I could. But—a whole year? I couldn't leave them that long, even if I wanted to."

"Now weren't you just telling me that you didn't want to take your sister's place?" Ilene took a step closer, and her voice lowered a little. "If they can't get along without you, haven't you done just that?"

"Oh, no." Magda swallowed hard and dropped her gaze. "Vi can take care of things perfectly well without me, of course—"

"Of course she can!" Ilene's tone brightened again. "The days of the spinster aunt are long over, and there's no reason in the world for a girl like you to hide away in a sleepy little town that can't make use of half your talent just because there aren't enough jobs to go around."

"Yes, but—"

"But what, Magdalen? You'd rather stay at home forever and be looked after like a child all your days just because your man hasn't come yet—and maybe never will?"

Magda sucked in a sharp breath that caught on a lump in her throat and turned to stare blindly through the car's spotless window. Ilene couldn't have any idea of the pain she was inflicting, but that didn't make it any less real.

"Just think what a help you could be to your family." Ilene continued speaking, apparently oblivious to the fact that she hadn't been given an answer. "You'd relieve them of the extra mouth they've been feeding for so long, and in the same stroke, you'd win them the car they never could have afforded. And you'd be helping me into the bargain. That is what you want most, isn't it? Or have I misunderstood you?"

"No." Magda finally managed to force the word past her aching throat. "I do want to help. It's a lovely idea, only—" Her voice cracked and broke, and in the next instant, Ilene's arm was around her shoulder.

"Oh, Magdalen, of course. Why, you've never been past Minneapolis, and here I am talking of hauling you from coast to coast and back again. Anyone would be homesick at the thought. That feeling doesn't last, you know. I can promise you it doesn't."

"Can you?" Magda looked up with a shimmer in her eyes, and Ilene squeezed her arm.

"I'll guarantee it. In fact, if you don't feel better after a week, I'll send you straight home. That's fair, isn't it?

And don't you think your family is worth a little sacrifice, when they've done so much for you?"

"Of course they are." Magda's words were still slightly choked, but she reached out a hand and laid it on top of the car, and Ilene stepped back with a smile.

"I knew you would think so. You'd happily take a job in town if it would help toward even a used car, wouldn't you? So why not this one that offers you so much more? And you won't fall off the face of the earth, for goodness' sake! Why, it'll be the most exciting thing in the world for the children to get postcards from all over the states. And you can even telephone them once or twice. You'll barely know you're away before you're back—and with more to show for it than anyone else could."

Magda lifted a hand to her shoulder as though instinctively reaching for a soft baby head, then slid it over to finger the gold chain with the single real teardrop pearl that the whole family had given her the previous Christmas.

"I would offer you time to think it over, Magdalen, but I really do need to be back on the road. I can give you another day to make your preparations if you're coming, but if you don't want this chance, please say so now. In that case, I'll drop you off in Homewood and continue on my way. Or if you can't bear my company any longer, I suppose your Jim would let you ride in his car—as long as it's still working."

HOME FOREVER

She paused for a beat, then turned and started back in the direction of her coupe, and Magda shot one quick glance back at the pristine wagon, then drew a fortifying breath and hurried after her.

ELEVEN

The picture of the bright new wagon next to Jim's old De Soto was the only thought that sustained Magda through that evening and the day that followed. Answering the cautious objections, anxious questions, and hesitant assurances from Violet and Jim was bad enough— yes, Ilene had offered references. No, she wanted to go, truly. Yes, of course she knew she'd always have a home with them. No, nothing had happened, but how could she resist a chance like this—to see the country and get paid for it besides?

She couldn't say a word about the car, of course, or the pain and fear that Ilene's well-chosen words had stirred, but since Violet and Jim kept any deeper concerns to the privacy of their own room and only voiced those that any conscientious sibling might raise, Magda managed to escape their scrutiny relatively unscathed.

But the next morning proved a different matter entirely. When Magda announced her plans at the breakfast table, there was a universal cry of dismay from the younger members of the family, not excepting baby Roxie, who had been unusually fussy all night and was likely getting her molars. Magda attempted to put the best possible face on her absence, promising them all as many postcards as she could manage and asking each one to think of something special she could find on her travels and send back for their birthdays, but the effort was a complete failure.

Len pressed her lips together hard and trained her eyes on her plate, and Ted pushed back his bowl and buried his head in his folded arms, nearly dousing his hair in milk and cereal. Bertie shot from her chair and hid herself in her mother's skirt, while Dale tugged at his father's arm and tearfully begged him to make her stay. Phyl's shrill "Don't go 'way, Magga!" that rose above Roxie's plaintive roars was the last straw, and Magda hurriedly excused herself to the kitchen, where she stood gripping the edge of the sink for long moments, battling the tears that would escape in spite of all she could do.

She sternly reminded herself that if she let this chance to help the family slip away, there would never be another like it; that Dale and Bertie's instinctive reaction toward Jim and Violet only proved how unnecessary her presence really was; that if she displayed anything less than excitement, the project would be doomed from the start. Then she dried her cheeks, sent up a desperate prayer for strength, and slowly returned to the dining room.

One glance around the table showed that Violet most certainly still had her household in hand, even in the wake of Magda's abject desertion. What she and Jim had told the children wasn't clear, but it had evidently served to quiet them, though little sniffs and hiccups still broke free from time to time.

When the meal was over and attention turned to preparations for her trip, Magda made sure to give each one a special task to help her with, and although none of the small faces regained quite its usual sparkle, the time spent together and the individual promises and minor tasks given in trust seemed to ease at least a bit of the children's tension. Violet was everywhere at once, thinking of all manner of little details that Magda would never have remembered, and Jim entirely disappeared for a few hours without explanation.

It wasn't until evening that Magda guessed the reason for his absence, and that only when she was presented with a knobby parcel—quite obviously a collection of several oddly shaped smaller packages—with the instruction that she was to store it safely in her luggage and not so much as peek at it until Christmas.

The thought of Christmas nearly overbalanced her carefully held restraint—why couldn't Ilene have waited just a few short weeks?—but the suspicious quiver in Ted's chin and the tear that slipped down Bertie's cheek had her throwing open the largest suitcase, declaring that if someone didn't help her find a place for the presents, she'd leave her galoshes behind. The ensuing rush and scramble was just as expected as Violet's firm declaration that she most certainly would *not*, and when the bag was finally re-packed, with both presents and galoshes safely stowed, it was nearly bedtime.

Never in the ten years since Magda and the children were alone upstairs had there been such a relentless patter of feet in the hall and creak of the squeaky hinge as there was that night. Violet's admonition, whatever it was, held good, and no word of complaint escaped, but there were a hundred confidences to be shared, and dozens of assurances to be given, and a few inevitable tears to be kissed away. But finally Magda was able to tuck the last curly head back under its covers and return to her own room, where she scooped up Roxie, whimpering softly in the crib, and settled into the old rocking chair before finally letting her own tears fall.

TWELVE

If not for church preparations, the next morning would have been utterly unbearable, but the usual round of ribbons and buttons and looking up lost shoes kept Magda busy enough that she hardly had time to think until she made a move to slip into the back of the old De Soto and Violet advised her quietly to take the front, so her dress wouldn't start the day rumpled. She crowded into the middle seat next to Ted with baby Roxie, leaving Magda with no choice but to follow instructions, swallow down her hollow feeling at the sight of Phyl cuddled up on Len's lap instead of her own, and try to ignore the sinking of her heart as the familiar home fell away behind her.

Even worse was the feeling when Jim parked the car next to the Haywoods' Plymouth and exited without a word to transfer Magda's suitcases to the trunk of the gleaming red Studebaker, which Ilene obligingly opened for him. It had been arranged that Magda would sit with Ilene in the back of the church so they could leave as soon as the service ended—Ilene had been willing to wait for the sermon, but not for what she called the interminable round of well-wishers that would be sure to follow it— so there was nothing left to do but say her final goodbyes.

An aching lump lodged in Magda's throat as she gazed over her family, looking unnaturally stiff and formal as they stood in front of Ilene, and abandoning all thought of wrinkles and the neighbors who had begun trickling into the church, she threw her arms wide and gathered close the little brood that immediately flung themselves at her. After a long, long hug in which more than one muffled sob could be heard, she freed herself from the clinging arms and touched cheeks, shoulders, and hair one at a time as she took in each woeful face.

"Len, darling, you'll be the best help Mother could ask for; I know you will. Teddy, dear, don't forget to find all the little ways to care for the family that a gentleman knows best. Bertie-bird, you'll help Phyllie with her buttons, won't you, and sing to her when she's scared in the night? Downy, remember to keep your things where they belong, and hold onto your smile, whatever you do. Phyl, dear, let Teddy and Bertie help you when Mother and Len are busy, and Roxie, darling, don't grow up too much while I'm gone, and don't forget me, will you?"

Her voice broke on the last word, and the next instant, Violet's free arm was crushing her close.

"You take care of yourself, darling. Have the most splendid time you can imagine. You've more than earned it. And don't worry about us. We'll be all right." Violet

66

wiped tears from her cheeks as she turned toward the church and motioned for the children to follow, and Jim stepped forward and slipped something into Magda's hand.

"Oh, Jim, don't! I can't." Magda's heart tore as she felt the rolled bills and guessed what they would mean for the family's little savings, but Jim shook his head firmly, though his voice stayed low.

"Keep it for emergencies. If you don't need it, you can give it back next Christmas. Maybe you have to go, but that doesn't mean I'm leaving you at the mercy of strangers."

It was beyond useless to argue, so Magda slipped the bills into her handbag, silently vowing that only the direst emergency would bring them out again. Then with a quick, firm squeeze of Jim's hand that she could only hope conveyed something of what her full heart refused to put into words, she moved back to Ilene's side as Jim's uneven stride carried him after Violet and the children.

"Well done, Magdalen." Ilene squeezed her arm, seeming to take no notice of the tears that were falling again. "We'll go in when the music begins and leave that way at the end, and then you'll be started on the grandest adventure of your life. I promise you it'll be worth it."

And with a lump still choking her throat, all Magda could do was nod as she watched the family climb the steps of the little white church and disappear inside.

THIRTEEN

"Number, please."

"Homewood 78." Magda gripped the receiver of the payphone with hands that were suddenly trembling, leaning forward in her eagerness. It had been more than two weeks since she'd left the little town, but even the sound of its name seemed to draw her heart toward it.

"I'm not familiar with that number, ma'am. Is this a San Francisco call?" the operator's voice questioned after a little pause, and Magda's cheeks flamed hot as she instinctively shook her head.

"Oh. No. Minnesota." Even alone in a telephone booth, there was no hiding the fact that she was completely out of her element, as every stop but the one on a sparsely-frequented Nevada road to repair a flat tire had amply proven.

"I'll give you long distance." The operator's voice clicked off to be replaced by another, who took what seemed an interminable length of time before naming an exorbitant price for the call.

Magda winced as she fed coin after coin into the slots on the telephone. Of course Ilene had been right; postcards were the only sensible way to communicate from a distance, and she would have to ration these indulgences much more carefully in the future. But a few scribbled words and a picture of the view could never substitute for everything she was missing, and the sight of a little Moravian star in the corner of a shop window had brought on such a strong wave of homesickness that she couldn't survive even one more night without talking to some of her dear ones. Even if Vi couldn't give her more than a minute—very possible if the children were elbow-deep in icing and colored sugars—just the sound of the happy activity would strengthen her to face her first Christmas all but alone in a bustling city.

"Go ahead, please." The operator's voice came back over the line, and Magda leaned in eagerly.

"Vi?"

"Aunt Magda?" The voice could almost have been Violet's except for the hesitant inflection. Had the girl grown that much in two short weeks, or was it merely a trick of the phone line?

"Len, darling, how are you? Where's Mother? How are all the Christmas plans coming?"

"Oh. Ah—" Len drew an odd little breath. "Mother's—just a bit busy now. Christmas…we put the tree up. The new star paper is really beautiful. I—"

70

"Len!" The cry was sharp and shrill enough to carry through the phone, and Len broke off with an abrupt "Just a minute, Aunt Magda."

There was a whispered conference on the other end of the line, of which Magda caught only "Teddy" before someone, likely Len, muffled the mouthpiece. After a few seconds, her voice came back again, more flustered than before.

"Aunt Magda, would—would you mind talking to Bertie for a minute? I need—I mean—I'll be right back."

Before Magda could even open her mouth, she was gone, and Bertie's hopeful little "Aunt Magda?" chirped on the other end of the line.

"How are you, Bertie-Bobby-bird? I've missed you so much, darling. Is everything all right?"

"I miss you too, Aunt Magda." The small voice wobbled just a little, and Magda thought she could hear a swallow before Bertie continued. "But I mean—not too much for you to worry." There was a second of silence as Magda tried to decipher this startling bit, then the little girl blurted abruptly, "I like your postcards!"

"I—I'm glad, darling. But listen, you shouldn't worry about me worrying. You can tell me anything, you know. That's what Aunt Magda is for, isn't it?"

"Yes, but Len said…" Bertie's voice trailed off, but before Magda could press further, a sharp gasp, a loud cry of "Phyllie, no!" and a distant crash rattled the line, followed by an abrupt thump and shrill, muffled scoldings as Bertie dropped the phone and ran toward the disaster.

FOURTEEN

Magda clutched the receiver tighter, trying to push away the awful fears that crowded in at the sounds of an unnamed accident too far away to reach. It could be nothing, of course; Phyl could have tried to undress Bertie's doll and then dropped it at the rebuke, or built a tower out of Jim's books and had it come crashing down, or tried to help Roxie walk and fallen on top of her. Where *were* Violet and Len?

"Aunt Magda?" It was not the quiet, capable voice she'd hoped to hear, but anything was better than that mysterious half-silence.

"Dale, dear, is everything all right? What did Phyllie do?"

"Oh." Dale's tone stayed unconcerned, and she could almost see his shrug. "I guess she wanted to make cookies herself. Or maybe eggs. Something with eggs. No-no, Roxie, stay here. Play truck. Or Bertie'll have to clean you up too."

Magda buried her face in her hand, then quickly pulled herself upright again. If poor Bertie was managing the cleanup, something more was wrong at home than a simple mishap with the eggs.

"Where's Mother, darling? Does she know about the mess?"

"Um, maybe. I guess she'll come when Daddy's better. No-no, Roxie. Dining room. Let's go there! Just a minute, Aunt Magda."

Magda clutched the receiver with white knuckles as she listened to the little grunts and bangs that signified Dale carrying the phone as he herded the baby into the dining room and away from the mess, praying that he wouldn't accidentally hit the plunger and sever the call completely.

"Good girl, Roxie." The muffled words were followed by a little sigh, and she could imagine Dale plopping himself on the ground next to the receiver. "It's okay now, Aunt Magda."

"Dale, what's wrong with Daddy?" Magda failed to keep the tremble out of her voice, but thankfully Dale didn't seem to notice.

"Um, his leg hurts lots. The car broke, and he was looking for olives for Mama, so all the other cars got back first, and he had to walk a long ways. That's why Mama said we have to be quiet and can't make cookies today, but I guess Phyl forgot."

The jumbled account would have been cryptic enough to an outsider, but Magda could read between the lines all too well. The car had broken down somewhere on the trip from Steadman back to Homewood, but Jim had been late already, and there had been no one else on the road to help. How far had he been forced to walk on his perpetually aching leg in the biting winter cold? Was there snow on the ground yet? And olives! There was only one time Vi craved olives enough to ask Jim to look for them if she couldn't find them at Hanby's. How long had she known? What other signs had Magda missed?

At least it explained where Violet was. But it still didn't account for Bertie being left to handle the mess.

"Where are Len and Teddy, darling?"

"Um, Teddy's in bed. I guess Len was taking him water. He's coughing lots."

"Teddy's sick?" Was the entire world back home crumbling? "Downy, what happened?"

"Mama says that's why you don't go out in slippers when it's twenty below, even to warm the car up for Daddy."

"Oh…" The word came out on a moan. Of course it would be Ted who shouldered that task when she left— dear, conscientious Teddy, with the biggest heart in the world and the weakest lungs in the family. How *could* she not have thought of it?

"Dale!" Even from a distance, she could hear Len's voice trembling on the edge of tears. "What are you telling her?" Her voice dropped, but she was close enough to the phone now that her words still carried. "Remember what Mother said? She's supposed to have a good time and not worry about us."

Dale protested something indistinct, but Len had the phone back to her mouth now and was speaking frantically.

"We're fine, Aunt Magda! It's—just a little—today isn't—"

"Len!" Bertie's plaintive cry held more than just the threat of tears, but before Magda could answer, another voice intruded.

"Your three minutes are up."

Magda dug frantically in her purse, but it was all too apparent that she didn't have nearly enough change to extend the call.

"Len, darling, I have to go. I love you all. Tell Mother—"

The phone clicked off.

FIFTEEN

"What on earth do you think you're doing?"

Magda ignored the sharp voice as she continued to pile things into her suitcases in a haphazard way that would have scandalized Violet. Only when the lid was unceremoniously shut and sat on did she even look up into Ilene's flashing eyes.

"I have to go home." Not since the red Starliner had left the limits of Homewood had five words felt so right. She ignored Ilene's sharp "Nonsense!" and turned to the smaller suitcase, until its lid was also slammed shut and leaned on, when she finally stood still and faced her companion. "You don't understand, Ilene. They need me! Teddy's sick, and Jim's leg kept him home today, and the car's quit again. Len's worn out, and Vi's expecting—"

"Good heavens, another?" Ilene threw up her hands, then slid off the suitcase and gripped Magda's shoulders hard. "Listen to me, Magdalen. You could have so much more from this world than rocking unconscionable numbers of infants and wrestling one ancient car off the scrap heap where it should have been long ago. Are you going to throw away everything I've done for you? Everything I've promised?"

"But don't you see?" Magda patted Ilene's hands and tried to slip around her, but the older woman blocked her path. "It's not the car they need. Not really. They need me. I'm sure of it now."

"Oh, of course they do!" Ilene's laugh was bitter. "What are you good for anyway besides coming at their every beck and call, giving up every scrap of a will of your own? I thought you had more sense than that, Magdalen. I must say I'm disappointed."

"I do have a will of my own." Magda crossed her arms and lifted her chin. "I know exactly what I want, and it's to catch the train to Chicago tomorrow morning and be back in Homewood by Christmas. You promised I could go if I wasn't happy, remember?"

"Oh, no." An icy smile touched the corners of Ilene's mouth, but she stepped back from the suitcases and let Magda continue her hurried packing. "That promise was for a week, not two and counting. You should have claimed it two Sundays ago if you wanted it."

Magda opened her mouth in an indignant gasp, but Ilene continued before she could speak.

"And before you ask me for your two weeks' 'pay,' I might as well remind you that our deal was the price of a car for a year's time—and a ridiculous piece of extravagance on my part. We never agreed to any kind of half pay, or anything at all if you didn't complete the full year. Which means if you leave now, you'll owe me the cost of all your meals and half the price of the hotel bills we've incurred to this point. Shall I write you an itemized bill?"

Magda turned abruptly back to the suitcases, biting her lip so hard she tasted blood as a frantic prayer for help rose in her heart.

"I suppose this is the thanks I should have expected for a girl from Nowhere, Minnesota." Ilene's tone was more suited to the chill of a northern winter than the un-seasonable warmth of San Francisco. "Shall I remind you just what I saved you from? Would you really prefer dec-ades more of drudgery in your sister's house, letting un-derqualified boys take the jobs you're infinitely more equipped for, waiting on a man who isn't coming?"

"Maybe he isn't." Magda spun around suddenly, and though her face was white to the lips, there was some-thing in her eyes that made Ilene take a step back. "But if he ever did, he would have taken my thoughts and feel-ings into account, not trampled them for his own pleas-ure—and the same goes for anyone who truly cares about me. We didn't agree to anything less than a year, so in the strictest terms, you don't owe me. But we also didn't agree to any responsibility on my part, so I don't owe you either. And if I do, you can deduct it from what you'd have paid for a tow and a patch job in Nevada and call it square. I don't owe you anything except thanks for your offer, but I *do* have a will of my own, and I'm exercising it now. I'm going home, and you can't stop me."

The long seconds of silence that followed Magda's emphatic declaration were unexpectedly broken by a low breath of laughter.

"Oh, Magdalen Morris, I *do* like you." Ilene sighed. "All right, we'll call it a draw. You don't owe me, and I don't owe you. But that doesn't change the fact that you're here without the means to go home, no matter how much you wanted to. Stick with me, and I'll make it worth your while, and get you home quicker than you'd make it if you managed to find a job in the city. Come now, forgive and forget?"

She stuck out a hand, smiling genially, and Magda studied her face for a moment before her shoulders slumped. She put her hand in Ilene's, and the older woman shook it quickly, her smile broadening.

"Good. Then unpack this mess and get dressed for the night. I'm taking you to dinner at Fisherman's Wharf."

"I don't think you understand, Ilene." Magda turned back to the bed and began stuffing the hems of her skirts inside the edges of the suitcase, sending up a silent blessing for Jim's provision and a pledge to Violet that she'd handle the next week's ironing herself. "I forgive you, but I'm not coming with you. Thankfully, there are some people in the world who still care more about me than about what I can give them—or cost them. I'm going home."

SIXTEEN

It was nearing midnight on Christmas Eve when a shabby little cab pulled to a stop in front of a snug Dutch Colonial on the very edge of Homewood. Magdalen Morris slid from the back seat and stood for a moment, drinking in the sight, as the cabbie removed her bags from the trunk and set them on the ground beside her. Then with a generous tip from the last of her own savings and a whispered "Merry Christmas," he was gone, and Magda lifted her suitcases and crept softly up the steps and into the vestibule, where she set down the luggage and hung her coat and hat on the peg that had been left empty far too long.

A light burned in the upstairs hallway and another in the kitchen, but a groan from the living room sent her steps in that direction, and the sight that met her eyes cracked her heart.

Jim sat on the floor with his head in his hands, leaning against the couch, which was turned with its back to the door, facing the Christmas tree. His artificial leg was no-where in sight, but a pair of crutches lay nearby, and the pieces of a boy's bicycle were spread in a hopeless mess before him. Dear Jim, who hadn't had a breath of a chance for the job at Pickett's because his fingers were all thumbs when it came to tools, whose leg must still hurt terribly if he had resorted to the hated crutches, sat here sacrificing his few precious hours of sleep to try to give Teddy more than a pile of parts and a promise for Christmas. How could she ever have thought they didn't need her?

"Instruction book need an instruction book again, Jim? It's a disgrace how they write those things, really." Magda slipped to her knees next to him, sweeping a handful of bolts into her lap, and Jim's head snapped up.

"Magda!" There was no mistaking the relief that struggled with amazement for supremacy in his tone. "What— How are you—"

"I'm just a plain small-town girl. I wasn't cut out for a world traveler, and I should've known it. Had to use your emergency money to get here for Christmas, but I'll pay it back as soon as I can. If you and Vi'll take me again."

"Magda…" The gentle reproof in his tone was answer enough for everything, but before he could say more, footsteps creaked on the stairs, and Jim held up a finger for silence.

"His fever's down some. I think he'll sleep a little while." The utter weariness in Violet's tone as she paused in the living room doorway wrenched Magda's heart, but her sister didn't seem to notice the figure kneeling in the shadows. "Jim, I never knew half how much I relied on Magda until now. I know it was right to let her go, but— I don't see how I'm going to get through the next few months without her."

"Come sit for a minute, Vi." A hint of concern dimmed the pleasure in Jim's eyes, but Violet shook her head.

"Not yet. I still have cinnamon rolls to make for to-morrow." She lifted a hand to her mouth, her face washing a shade paler in the half light. Jim reached for his crutches, but Violet waved him back. "Don't. I'm all right."

"You come rest and let someone else handle the cinnamon rolls." Jim shot a glance at Magda, who nodded and smiled as she set the bolts silently back on the floor again.

"I wouldn't be any better with the bike, and you know it. And the only thing worse than making them myself would be cleaning up after *your* attempts to make them."

The weak attempt at humor brought a tender smile to Magda's lips as she rose from the floor and moved out of the shadows.

"How about my cinnamon rolls, Vi? They're nothing compared to yours, I know, but—"

"Magda!" Violet gave one startled gasp before bursting into tears and weeping into her sister's neck. Magda held her for a long minute, then drew her over to the couch, wiping tears from her own eyes as Violet dried her cheeks. "Magda, what are you— How did you— Oh, I shouldn't have said all that! We're all right, darling, truly—"

"Don't, Vi." Magda laughed shakily as she rested her head against her sister's shoulder. "I found out I'm a homebody through and through. At least let me believe I'm a little bit useful."

"Oh, Magda." Violet's voice quivered, and Magda slid back to the floor with the old merry twinkle sparkling in her eyes.

"I've been sitting around trains and cabs and stations for more days than I'd like to count, and I'm absolutely aching for something to do. So I'm going to wrestle this bike into submission and then I'm going to mix up a batch of cinnamon rolls, and the two of you can either go to bed or stay up and watch, but you'd best park yourselves on the couch and out of my way. Put your feet up, Vi; you and the baby have been doing too much, I can tell."

"How did you even know?" Violet curled her feet up obediently as Jim awkwardly lifted himself to the couch beside her and Magda picked up a set of handlebars. "I only told Jim yesterday."

"Olives, Vi. Blame the olives." Magda glanced over at the tree, with its paper Moravian stars in all different levels of child craftsmanship hung carefully on the branches, and her smile softened. "And thank the Lord."

SEVENTEEN

Hours later, Magda finally crept upstairs with her full suitcases, minus the presents that now sat in their proper place under the tree. A bright new bike stood covered in blankets next to them, and two pans of cinnamon rolls kept warm in the oven. Jim and Violet had retired to their room for what rest they could get, and the house lay in silence, waiting for Dale or Phyllis to wake to the realization that it was Christmas morning and no time to lie in bed.

Magda set the bags in the hallway and peeped into her own room through the door Ellen had left open. The girl lay on her bed with Roxie's little cloth doll clenched in her fist, the lines on her face creased uneasily, even in sleep. Darling Len, who worked so hard, worried so much, and did more than enough for her mother during the day—she shouldn't have to feel the full weight of responsibility for her siblings at night. Magda quietly slid the suitcases into the room where Len's eyes would fall on them first thing, gave one light stroke to Roxie's soft hair, then crept to the girls' room.

Len's bed was empty, of course, but the sight of Phyllis's vacant covers made her heart skip until she spotted the two small heads cuddled together in Bertie's bed. The dears! Had Phyllie had a nightmare as she sometimes did? Or was it the loneliness of the room without Len's steadying presence that had affected them? Magda tucked a peppermint into the pocket of each little robe and draped Phyl's across the foot of Bertie's bed, then blew two kisses before she left the room.

As she started for the last door, the sound of coughing turned her toward the stairs and down to the kitchen for a glass of water instead. When she returned to the boys' room and eased the door open, Dale was asleep in the nearest bed, spread-eagle in his usual fashion, with half his covers kicked off. Magda pulled them back over him and stole to the other bed, where Teddy was still coughing intermittently, curled up in a miserable heap with his face to the wall. A chair had been pulled close to the bedside and the little table stripped of its boyish clutter to make space for medicine bottles, thermometer, handkerchief, and the twin to her glass, now dry and comfortless.

"Here, Teddy, darling, drink this." Magda kept her voice to a whisper as she slipped into the chair and smoothed his hair back. Ted blinked at her for a second, then sat bolt upright and clasped his arms around her neck, his hoarse "Aunt Magda!" barely audible amid the coughing fit that seized him. Magda held him, hushed him, made him drink, and finally slipped a peppermint between his lips. A look of pure bliss spread over the boy's face as he sucked it.

"It's not a dream." A weak cough escaped him, and he nestled closer into Magda's shoulder, his face warm against her neck. "Oh, Aunt Magda. You came home for Christmas?"

"Oh, no, not for Christmas, Teddy." Tears swam in Magda's eyes as she cuddled him close and pressed a kiss to his hair. "This time, I'm home forever."

Publisher's Cataloging-in-Publication data

Names: Thompson, Angie, author.
Title: Home forever / by Angie Thompson.
Description: Lynchburg, Virginia : Quiet Waters Press, 2023. |
Summary: When a rich stranger offers Magda an unusual chance
to help her family, she discovers just how much she is needed and
valued.
Identifiers: ISBN 9781951001308 (epub) | ISBN 9781951001315
(pbk)
Subjects: LCSH: Christmas stories, American. | Families—Fic-
tion. | Aunts—Fiction. | BISAC: FICTION / Holidays.
Classification: LCC PS3620.H649 H66 2023